The ZILLIONAIRE'S DAUGHTER

BY EDWARD SOREL

1248 1526

WARNER
JUVENILE
BOOKS

A Warner Communications Company

New York

For Saskia, Andrew, Teddy, Halley, and Isaac,
and all the other children born too late
to travel on the *S.S. Gigantic.*

Warner Juvenile Books Edition
Copyright © 1989 by Edward Sorel
All rights reserved.

Warner Books, Inc., 666 Fifth Avenue, New York, NY 10103

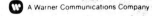 A Warner Communications Company

Printed in the United States of America
First Warner Juvenile Books Printing: November 1989
10 9 8 7 6 5 4 3 2 1

Library of Congress Cataloging-in-Publication Data

Sorel, Edward, date.
     The zillionaire's daughter / Edward Sorel.
          p. cm.
     Summary: A french zillionaire and his daughter cross the Atlantic
in the *S.S. "Gigantic,"* where she finds her unexpected destiny.
     ISBN: 1-55782-120-8
     [1. Ships—Fiction.   2. Stories in rhyme.]   I. Title.
PZ8.3.S714Zi   1989
[E]—dc20   88–40621
                                                                          CIP
                                                                          AC

At home in his favorite vermillion chair
Sat Max Maximillion, the French zillionaire,
Exhausted from working all day at his chore
Of buying for less and then selling for more.

Max nodded off, but awoke in a hurry—
On top of his head he could feel something furry!
Then Max heard a giggle and knew it was Claire,
His mischievous daughter, in back of his chair.

They laughed and they laughed until tears filled their eyes.
"I, too," announced Max, "have a little surprise.
In a very few days we will cross the Atlantic
On my luxury liner, the *S.S. Gigantic*."

On the way to the dock in their yellow Renault,
They got caught in bad traffic (which wasn't their fault).
By the time they arrived they were three hours late,
But since Max owned the ship—well, the ship had to wait.

Some newsmen had gathered to ask Max his views;
There was even a camera from Movietone News.
A reporter stopped Claire: "*S'il-vous-plait*, won't you tell—
Was your outfit designed by Coco Chanel?"

They walked up the gangplank; the ship's whistle tooted.
The Captain stepped forward and smartly saluted.
Max took down the sign that said NO DOGS ALLOWED
So that Claire's puppy Jacques would feel part of the crowd.

From the uppermost deck, Papa Max, Claire and Jacques
Waved happy good-byes to the folks on the dock.
Then Claire got impatient (which was perfectly normal)
To change into clothes just a little less formal.

While taking a stroll both starboard and port,
They happened to pass by a shuffleboard court.
Claire won seven games before Max said, "Now listen,
I just can't go on, dear. I'm not in condition."

Claire then suggested a dip in the pool,
But her father considered the air much too cool.
He had the ship take a more southerly route,
And Claire took a swim in her new bathing suit.

At dinner they sat at the Captain's own table.
The men wore tuxedos; the women wore sable.
The seating arrangement placed Claire in between
Her father and someone she'd seen on the screen.

At Max's right hand sat the Countess von Zeller,
A world-famous psychic (that means fortune-teller).
Max asked her if later she'd look at Claire's hand
To study her lifeline and see what fate planned.

One look and the Countess turned gray, and then grayer.
"Your daughter will marry a saxophone player!"
"A saxophone player!" cried Max in a huff.
"That's simply absurd! I've heard quite enough!"

Still later that evening with Claire safe in bed,
Max stared out the porthole, his heart filled with dread.
"My daughter should marry a man of position,
Not a saxophone player, a lowly musician!"

Poor Max! He had such a terrible night!
But Claire was up early, before it was light.
On deck she met Charlie and found that, though English,
He spoke perfect French (the young man was bi-linguish).

From that morning on they were always together,
Exploring the ship, whatever the weather,
From the stem to the stern and from rigging to gearing,
And sometimes the Captain let them do the steering.

So nine days went by on the *S.S. Gigantic*.
Then the ladies and gentlemen all became frantic,
Concocting their costumes (some borrowed, some made)
For the last night at sea—the Grand Masquerade.

A pirate escorted a queen with a train.
A clown threw confetti. A cat drank champagne.
And when the band played the song "I Got Rhythm,"
There were Charlie and Claire dancing right along with 'em.

They lindy-ed and boogie-ed—the crowd begged for more,
But Charlie had other surprises in store.
He jumped on the bandstand and borrowed a sax,
And everyone cheered (except, of course, Max)—

Because Claire's buddy Charlie, in spite of his size,
Blew on that sax just like one of the guys.
Max turned to the Captain. "Say, who is this Charlie?"
"Don't you know?" he replied. "He's the third Duke of Harley."

Then Max understood it was silly to get
Upset about things that had not happened yet.
Next day when they docked, the young duke and Claire
Planned a reunion at the New York World's Fair.

And that's just what happened. They met at the Fair—
The Grand Duchess of Harley, Max, Charlie and Claire.
And there they had tea at the vermillion pavilion—
The Duchess, Claire, Charlie and Max Maximillion.